Praise for
Disgraced

"The best play I saw last year....A quick-witted and shattering
drama....*Disgraced* rubs all kinds of unexpected raw spots with
intelligence and humor."   —Linda Winer, *Newsday*

"A sparkling and combustible contemporary drama....Ayad
Akhtar's one-act play deftly mixes the political and personal,
exploring race, freedom of speech, political correctness, even the
essence of Islam and Judaism. The insidery references to the
Hamptons and Bucks County, Pennsylvania, and art critic Jerry
Saltz are just enough to make audience members feel smart....
Akhtar...has lots to say about America and the world today. He
says it all compellingly, and none of it is comforting."
                    —Philip Boroff, *Bloomberg Businessweek*

"Compelling....*Disgraced* raises and toys with provocative and
nuanced ideas."   —Jesse Oxfeld, *New York Observer*

"A continuously engaging, vitally engaged play about thorny questions of identity and religion in the contemporary world....In dialogue that bristles with wit and intelligence, Mr. Akhtar...puts
contemporary attitudes toward religion under a microscope, reveal-
ing how tenuous self-image can be for people born into one way of
being who have embraced another....Everyone has been told that
politics and religion are two subjects that should be off-limits at
social gatherings. But watching Mr. Akhtar's characters rip into
these forbidden topics, there's no arguing that they make for ear-
tickling good theater."   —Charles Isherwood, *New York Times*

"A blistering social drama about the racial prejudices that secretly persist in progressive cultural circles."

—Marilyn Stasio, *Variety*

"Terrific....*Disgraced*...unfolds with speed, energy and crackling wit....The evening will come to a shocking end, but before that, there is the sparkling conversation, expertly rendered on the page by Akhtar....Talk of 9/11, of Israel and Iran, of terrorism and airport security, all evokes uncomfortable truths. Add a liberal flow of alcohol and a couple of major secrets suddenly revealed, and you've got yourself one dangerous dinner party....In the end, one can debate what the message of the play really is. Is it that we cannot escape our roots, or perhaps simply that we don't ever really know who we are, deep down, until something forces us to confront it? Whatever it is, when you finally hear the word 'disgraced' in the words of one of these characters, you will no doubt feel a chill down your spine." —Jocelyn Noveck, Associated Press

"Offers an engaging snapshot of the challenge for upwardly mobile Islamic Americans in the post-9/11 age."

—Thom Geier, *Entertainment Weekly*

"Akhtar digs deep to confront uncomfortable truths about the ways we look at race, culture, class, religion, and sex in this bracingly adult, unflinching drama....He writes incisive, often quite funny dialogue and creates vivid characters, managing to cover a lot of ground in a mere four scenes and 80 minutes. Akhtar doesn't offer any solutions to the thorny issues he presents so effectively. What he does is require us to engage them, and that's a very good and necessary thing." —Erik Haagensen, Backstage.com

"*Disgraced* stands among recent marks of an increasing and welcome phenomenon: the arrival of South Asian and Middle Eastern Americans as presences in our theater's dramatis personae, matching their presence in our daily life. Like all such phenomena, it carries a double significance. An achievement and a sign of recognition for those it represents, for the rest of us it constitutes the theatrical equivalent of getting to know the new neighbors—something we had better do if we plan to survive as a civil society."

—Michael Feingold, *Village Voice*

ALSO BY AYAD AKHTAR

American Dervish

Disgraced

A PLAY

AYAD AKHTAR

BACK BAY BOOKS
Little, Brown and Company
New York   Boston   London

For Amanda, P.J., Kimberly & Paige

Back Bay Books / Little, Brown and Company
Hachette Book Group
1290 Avenue of the Americas, New York, NY 10104
littlebrown.com

First edition: September 2013

Back Bay Books is an imprint of Little, Brown and Company. The Back Bay Books name and logo are trademarks of Hachette Book Group, Inc.

The publisher is not responsible for websites (or their content) that are not owned by the publisher.

The Hachette Speakers Bureau provides a wide range of authors for speaking events. To find out more, go to hachettespeakersbureau.com or call (866) 376-6591.

ISBN 978-0-316-32446-5
Library of Congress Control Number 2013946485

15

LSC-C

Printed in the United States of America

ON READING PLAYS

Plays on the page are neither fish nor fowl. A play is seldom meant to be read. It is meant to be pored over, interrogated, dissected, obeyed. A play is a blueprint, a workman's plan drawn for a group of collaborating artists, and it must contain the seeds of inspiration, the insinuations of truth that will spur the actors and the director and the designers handily to tell the playwright's chosen tale. The end result of the process that begins with a play is not the encounter with an individual reader in the privacy of a moment, but rather the boisterous and public encounter with a living audience, an act of collective hearing and seeing that is at the root of the theater's timeless and ritual magic.

There can still be a magic to the reader's silent encounter with dialogue on a page. This encounter can have the thrill of over-heard conversation, the piecing together of circumstance, situation, emotion, the making sense of what we cannot see. These are pleasures of incompleteness, for *incomplete* is what reading a play can feel like to someone more accustomed to the fullness of a novel. To be sure, a book does call upon the reader to complete the mental picture, but the truth is that a novel gives you more. It must. The novelist uses words alone—not lights or actors or the semblances of places—to cast the story's spell. Some novelists will amass the details, others will be sparing. But however little you may think to find by way of depiction in even the most economical of novels, rest assured, you will find so much less in even the most voluble of plays.

The wonder of reading a play has to do with what dialogue offers and what it denies. Shakespeare says little about his settings. Plainly announced before the play has begun, the particulars emerge through the course of what follows, through the revelations of dialogue. Our sense of the castle in Elsinore where Hamlet's fate is being decided comes to us from the characters' mouths. Indeed, in Shakespeare, description is never simply his own; it is always colored by the psychology and circumstance of the one speaking his words. Outer landscape is the reflection of an inner state, and everything the characters say reveals to us their hearts and minds.

It is true that everything in a play *operates*—or at least should. It is an exacting form. The plot must move, and the words must move it. There is time for digression, as long as digression reveals the depths and subtleties that give the work its distinction, its reason for being. Such economy yields a different sort of interiority than the wondrous—and often encyclopedic—inner current that can run between novelist and reader. In a play, the words are signals; they announce and evoke; as building blocks of a plan, they do not consummate, but rather promise; they direct, conceal, uncover.

On the page, the language of a play can seem to be pointing always to a kind of absence. After all, so much is missing: the actors, the set, the audience. What's more, in the finest plays, it seems that the dialogue never quite speaks the hidden truth, never quite articulates the central emotion, but only talks around such things, leaving space for the audience to complete the connection. It is a form that thrives on omission, which is why reading a play can have something of the thrill of detective work, clues emerging line by line, slowly rounding out the picture that is the deeper reason for the play itself.

Absence, then, is the reigning principle of a written play, and even its very form on the page—mostly white space—serves as invitation for the reader. It is a blankness that points the way not only to the empty space of the stage on which the story will eventually unfold, but, well before this can ever happen, to that bareness of a reader's mind, awaiting, expectant, eager for the pleasure of shared imagination to begin.

PRODUCTION
HISTORY

Disgraced had its world premiere on January 30, 2012, at American Theater Company, Chicago, Illinois (PJ Paparelli, Artistic Director). It was directed by Kimberly Senior; the set design was by Jack Magaw; the costume design was by Janice Pytel; the lighting design was by Christine Binder; the sound design was by Kevin O'Donnell; and the stage manager was Katie Klemme. The cast was as follows:

AMIR...Usman Ally
EMILY...Lee Stark
ABE...Behzad Dabu
ISAAC...Benim Foster
JORY...Alana Arenas

Disgraced received its New York premiere by Lincoln Center Theater / LCT3 (André Bishop, Artistic Director; Bernard Gersten, Executive Director; Paige Evans, Artistic Director / LCT3) on October 22, 2012. It was directed by Kimberly Senior; the set design was by Lauren Helpern; the costume design was by Dane Laffrey; the lighting design was by Tyler Micoleau; the sound design was by Jill BC Du Boff; the stage manager was Megan

Schwarz Dickert; the managing director was Adam Siegel; and the production manager was Jeff Hamlin. The cast was as follows:

AMIR...Aasif Mandvi
EMILY...Heidi Armbruster
ABE...Omar Maskati
ISAAC...Erik Jensen
JORY...Karen Pittman

Disgraced received its U.K. premiere at London's Bush Theatre (Madani Younis, Artistic Director; Sian Alexander, Executive Director) on May 22, 2013. The production was directed by Nadia Fall; the set and costume design were by Jaimie Todd; the lighting design was by James Whiteside; the sound design was by Mike Walker; the stage manager was Harriet Stewart. The cast was as follows:

AMIR...Hari Dhillon
EMILY...Kirsty Bushell
ABE...Danny Ashok
ISAAC...Nigel Whitmey
JORY...Sara Powell

Disgraced

Setting

A spacious apartment on New York's Upper East Side.

Time

2011–2012.

The first two scenes take place in late summer of 2011.

The third scene takes place three months later during fall.

The fourth scene takes place six months later during spring.

The play should be performed without intermission.

Scene One

Lights come up.

High ceilings, parquet floors, crown molding. The works.

Upstage—a dining table. Behind it, a swinging door leads to a kitchen.

Upstage right—an open doorway leads to a hall that disappears from view.

Upstage left—a terrace and windows looking out over further buildings in the distance. Through which the season will show in each scene.

Downstage—a living room. A couch and chairs gathered together around a coffee table.

The stage left wall is covered with a large painting: A vibrant, two-paneled image in luscious whites and blues, with patterns reminiscent of an Islamic garden. The effect is lustrous and magnetic.

Below, a marble fireplace. And on the mantel, a statue of Siva. Along one or more of the walls, bookshelves.

To one side, a small table on which a half-dozen bottles of alcohol sit.

Downstage right—a vestibule and the front door.

(The furnishings are spare and tasteful. Perhaps with subtle flourishes of the Orient.)

On stage: Emily—early 30s, white, lithe and lovely—sits at the end of the dining table. A large pad before her and a book open to a large reproduction of Velázquez's Portrait of Juan de Pareja.

Emily assesses her model…

Amir—40, of South Asian origin, in an Italian suit jacket and a crisp, collared shirt, but only boxers underneath. He speaks with a perfect American accent.

Posing for his wife.

She sketches him. Until…

AMIR: You sure you don't want me to put pants on?

EMILY *(Showing the Velázquez painting)*: I only need you from the waist up.

AMIR: I still don't get it.

EMILY: You said it was fine.

AMIR: It is fine. It's just…

EMILY: What?

AMIR: The more I think about it…

EMILY: Mmm-hmm.

AMIR: I think it's a little weird. That you want to paint me after seeing a painting of a slave.

EMILY: He was Velázquez's assistant, honey.

AMIR: His slave.

EMILY: Until Velázquez freed him.

AMIR: Okay.

EMILY: I mean how many times have we stopped in front of that painting?

AMIR: It's a good painting. No idea what it has to do with what happened last night. I mean, the guy was a dick.

EMILY: He wasn't just a dick. He was a dick to you. And I could tell why.

AMIR: Honey, it's not the first time—

EMILY: A man, a waiter, looking at you.

AMIR: Looking at us.

EMILY: Not seeing you. Not seeing who you really are. Not until you started to deal with him. And the deftness with which you did that. You made him see that gap. Between what he was assuming about you and what you really are.

AMIR: The guy's a racist. So what?

EMILY: Sure. But I started to think about the Velázquez painting. And how people must have reacted when they first saw it. They think they're looking at a picture of a Moor. An assistant.

AMIR: A slave.

EMILY: Fine. A slave.

But whose portrait—it turns out—has more nuance and complexity than his renditions of kings and queens. And God knows how many of those he painted.

AMIR: You know what I think? I think you should just call your black Spanish boyfriend and get him up here to sit for you. He's still in New York, isn't he?

EMILY: Honey, I have no idea.

AMIR: You don't have to rub it in, babe.

I know all men are not created equal—

7

EMILY *(Gesturing for him to take the pose)*: Could you do the thing?

AMIR *(Adjusting his arm)*: Way to make a guy feel wanted—

   If anything, I guess I should be grateful to José, right? Broke your dad in. I mean at least I spoke English.

EMILY: Dad's still traumatized. He brought up that Thanksgiving on the phone the other day.

   (Assessing her sketch)

   Anyway—I don't know what you're so worried about. It's not like anybody's gonna see this.

AMIR: Baby. Jerry Saltz loved your last show.

EMILY: He liked it. He didn't love it. It didn't sell.

AMIR: Selling's not everything.

   Amir's cell phone RINGS.

EMILY: Selling's not everything? You really believe that?

   Emily grabs the phone and tosses it to him.

AMIR: It's a client...

EMILY: Fine. Just...stay where you are?

AMIR *(Into the phone)*: What?

   (Listening)

   Paolo, I'm not your therapist. You don't pay me to listen to you. You pay me to listen to me.

   Yeah, but you're not listening.

   You're going. To kill. This deal.

   (Emily approaches, to adjust him)

   Honey...

   (Continuing into the phone)

   The point is, they buy it? They own it.

   They do what they want. That's how it works.

(Checking...)

Paolo. I'm getting another call. It's about the contract. I gotta go.

(Switching over)

You enjoying your Cheerios?

Well, what the fuck else was keeping you from calling me back?

I don't care that it's Saturday morning. You're paid six figures to return my calls.

(Breaking away and going to a contract on the table)

Paragraph four, subsection three. Last sentence.

Why are those three words still in there?

You missed that? No. What actually happened is I told you to fix it and you didn't.

Then behave like it.

(Hanging up)

Fucking career paralegal.

EMILY: Wow.

AMIR: I don't catch his little fuck-up? It costs the client eight hundred fifty grand.

EMILY *(Sketching)*: It's actually kinda hot.

AMIR *(Coming over to see the sketch over her shoulder)*: You're so good.

(Pointing at the picture of the Velázquez painting)

What's his name again?

EMILY: Juan de Pareja.

AMIR: It's a little fucked up. Give me that at least.

EMILY *(Sexy)*: I happen to know you like it a little fucked up.

They kiss.

AMIR: I should call Mort.

EMILY *(As Amir punches numbers)*: You want more coffee?

Amir nods. Emily exits.

AMIR *(Into the phone)*: Hey, Mort...

Good, good. So listen, I talked to Paolo again.

Seller's remorse.

It's a moot point. His board's gonna vote against him.

What do you want me to do?

Okay. I'll feed him the line on litigation. He doesn't have the stomach for that. By the time I'm through with him, he'll go into PTSD every time he sees my name on his caller ID.

Emily returns with coffee.

AMIR (CONT'D): She's right here...

(To Emily)

Mort says hi.

EMILY: Tell him hi.

AMIR: She says hi...

We have plans for Labor Day, Mort.

Don't worry about it. Enjoy the weekend...

Sounds good. See you then.

EMILY: Hamptons?

AMIR: Honey, Jory and Isaac.

Bucks County.

It's taken forever to make that happen...

EMILY: I know, I know.

It's got me a little freaked out. Isaac's a big deal.

AMIR: And he is going to love your work.

EMILY: How is Mort?

AMIR: Obsessed with the idea that meditation is going to bring down his cholesterol.

EMILY: Haven't seen him in ages.

AMIR: I barely see him. He hardly comes in. A couple of hours a day at most when he does show up.

EMILY: Pays to be the boss.

AMIR: I mean, basically, I'm doing his job. I don't mind.

EMILY: He loves you.

AMIR: He depends on me.

EMILY: Okay.

He spent I don't know how much on that birthday present for you?

AMIR: Couple grand at least.

EMILY: Excuse me.

AMIR: Honey, I really am pretty much doing his job.

EMILY: So he gets you a book. Or a bottle of scotch. Or takes you to dinner.

Why'd he get you a statue of Siva?

(Beat)

He doesn't think you're Hindu, does he?

AMIR: He may have mentioned something once...

You realize I'm going to end up with my name on that firm?

EMILY: Leibowitz, Bernstein, Harris, and Kapoor.

AMIR: My mother will roll over in her grave...

EMILY: Your mother would be proud.

AMIR: It's not the family name, so she might not care, seeing it alongside all those Jewish ones...

From the kitchen: the intercom BUZZES.

*Amir looks over, surprised. Emily puts down her pencil.
Heads for the kitchen.*

EMILY: That'll be Abe.

AMIR *(Surprised)*: Abe?

EMILY *(Disappearing into the kitchen)*: Your nephew?

AMIR: Oh, right. Wait...

EMILY *(At the intercom, off stage)*: Yes?

Send him up.

As Emily now returns...

AMIR: You're not gonna let this thing go, are you?

EMILY: I don't like what's happening. Somebody's gotta do something about it.

AMIR: I went to see that guy in prison. What more do you two want?

There's a KNOCKING on the door.

Amir puts on his pants on his way to the door.

He opens it. To find...

ABE—22, of South Asian origin. But as American as American gets. Vibrant and endearing. He's wearing a Kidrobot T-shirt under a hoodie, skinny jeans, and high-tops.

As Amir is buckling his belt.

ABE *(Looking over at Emily, back to Amir)*: Should I come back?

AMIR: No, no.

ABE: You sure?

AMIR: Yeah. I'm sure. Come in, Hussein.

ABE: Uncle.

AMIR: What?

ABE: Could you just call me—

AMIR *(Finishing his thought)*: I've known you your whole life as Hussein. I'm not gonna start calling you Abe now.

Abe shakes his head. Turning to Emily.

EMILY: Hi, Abe.

ABE: Hi, Aunt Emily.

Abe turns to Amir, lighthearted.

ABE (CONT'D) *(Pointing)*: See? How hard can it be?

AMIR: Abe Jensen?
        Really?

ABE: You know how much easier things are for me since I changed my name? It's in the Quran. It says you can hide your religion if you have to.

AMIR: I'm not talking about the Quran. I'm talking about you being called Abe Jensen.
        Just lay off it with me and your folks at least.

ABE: It's gotta be one thing or the other. I can't be all mixed up.

EMILY *(Off Amir's reaction)*: Amir. You changed your name, too.

ABE: You got lucky.
        You didn't have to change your first name.
        Could be Christian. Jewish.
        Plus, you were born here. It's different.

EMILY: You want something, sweetie? Coffee, juice?

ABE: Nah. I'm good.

AMIR: So what's up?

EMILY: I'll let you gentlemen talk.

AMIR: No need. Everybody knows you're in on this.

(To Abe)

So you've been calling her, too?

ABE: You weren't calling me back.

AMIR: Why are we still talking about this?

I'm a corporate lawyer. In mergers and acquisitions—

EMILY: Who started in the public defender's—

AMIR: That was years ago.

(Beat)

Your man should have been more careful…

ABE: Imam Fareed didn't do anything.

Every church in the country collects money. It's how they keep their doors open. We're entitled, too.

He's running a mosque—

EMILY: He's got the right.

Just because they're collecting money doesn't mean it's for Hamas.

AMIR: What does any of this have to do with me?

EMILY: It doesn't matter to you that an innocent man is in prison?

AMIR: I don't know Patriot Act law. The guy's already got a legal team. Those guys Ken and Alex are amazing.

ABE: They're not Muslim.

AMIR: There we go.

ABE: What?

AMIR: What I thought.

I'm not gonna be part of a legal team just because your imam is a bigot.

ABE: He's not a bigot. He'd just be more comfortable if there was a Muslim on the case, too…

AMIR: More comfortable if he wasn't being represented by a couple of Jews?

ABE: No.

AMIR: Really?

ABE *(Beat)*: He liked you. He said you were a good man.

AMIR: Well, he might not feel the same if he knew how I really felt about his religion.

ABE *(Offhand)*: That's just a phase.

AMIR *(Taken aback)*: Excuse me?

ABE: That's what Mom says Grandma used to say about you. That you were working something out. That you were such a good Muslim when you were a kid. And that you had to go the *other way* for a while.

AMIR *(Dumbfounded)*: The *other way*?
(Considering)
   Sit down, Hussein. I want to tell you something.

ABE: So just tell me.

AMIR: No. I want you to sit down.

Abe sits.

AMIR (CONT'D): When was the first time you had a crush?

ABE: I thought you wanted to tell me something.

AMIR: I'm getting to it.
   Your first crush...

ABE *(Glancing at Emily)*: Umm...
   Fifth grade. A girl named Nasleema...

AMIR: I was in sixth.
   Her name was Rivkah.

EMILY: I thought your first crush was Susan.

AMIR: That was the first girl I ever kissed. Rivkah was the first girl I ever got up in the morning thinking about. One time she went away to Disney World for a week, and I was *a mess.* Didn't even want to go to school if I couldn't see her.

(Remembering)

She was a looker. Dark hair, dark eyes. Dimples. Perfect white skin.

EMILY: Why didn't you ever tell me about her?

AMIR: I didn't want you to hate my mother...

(Off Emily's perplexed look)

Just wait...

(Back to Abe)

So Rivkah and I'd gotten to the point where we were trading notes. And one day, my mother found one of the notes.

Of course it was signed, Rivkah.

Rivkah? my mom says. *That's a Jewish name.*

(Beat)

I wasn't clear on what exactly a Jew was at the time, other than they'd stolen land from the Palestinians, and something about how God hated them more than other people...

I couldn't imagine God could have hated this little girl.

So I tell my mom, *No, she's not Jewish.*

But she knew the name was Jewish.

If I ever hear that name in this house again, Amir, she said, *I'll break your bones. You will end up with a Jew over my dead body.*

Then she spat in my face.

EMILY: My God.

AMIR: *That's so you don't ever forget,* she says.

Next day?

Rivkah comes up to me in the hall with a note. *Hi, Amir,* she says. Eyes sparkling.

I look at her and say, *You've got the name of a Jew.*

She smiles. *Yes, I'm Jewish,* she says.

(Beat)

Then *I* spit in *her* face.

EMILY: That's horrible.

ABE: Man. That's effed up.

AMIR: So, when my older sister goes on to you about *this way* and the *other way,* now you'll have a better idea of the *phase* I'm really going through...

It's called *intelligence.*

Pause.

EMILY: I'm surprised.

AMIR: By what?

EMILY: I don't know. Your mother was very open with me...

AMIR: Let's just say I made it abundantly clear not to mess with you.

EMILY: I thought she liked me.

ABE: Seemed like it to me.

EMILY: She kissed me on her deathbed.

AMIR: You won her over. You were openhearted, gracious.

EMILY: You make it sound like there was some whole battle going on.

AMIR: Well...

EMILY: About what?

AMIR: White women have no self-respect.

How can someone respect themselves when they think they have to take off their clothes to make people like them?

They're whores.

EMILY: What are you saying?

AMIR: What Muslims around the world say about white women—

ABE *(Coming in)*: Not everyone says that.

AMIR: Have you heard it or not?

ABE: Yeah.

AMIR: And more than once?

ABE: Yes.

AMIR: And from your mother?

Abe nods.

AMIR (CONT'D): I rest my case.

Pause.

ABE: Imam Fareed is not like that. If you got to know him better, you'd realize. He's actually your kind of guy. Once a month, we're doing a Friday prayer that's mixed.

EMILY: And—he let me sit in his mosque and sketch every day for weeks.

AMIR: He was probably hoping you'd convert. Who knows, you probably will.

EMILY: Don't be dismissive.

AMIR: I don't understand what you see in it.

EMILY: In what?

AMIR: In Islam?

EMILY: When we were in the mosque in Cordoba...Remember that? The pillars and arches?

AMIR: Those were great.

EMILY: Remember what you said?

AMIR: I'm sure you're going to remind me.

EMILY: That it actually made you feel like praying.

AMIR: That's kind of the point of a mosque, honey.

EMILY: And that Matisse show you loved so much? He got all that from Mogul miniatures. Carpets. Moroccan tiles.

AMIR: Fine. I got it.

EMILY: There's so much beauty and wisdom in the Islamic tradition. Look at Ibn Arabi, Mulla Sadra —

AMIR *(Coming in abruptly)*: But the thing is? It's not just beauty and wisdom.

Pause.

ABE: Uncle. Don't think of him as a Muslim if you don't want to. Just think of him as a wise man. Who so many people depend on.

AMIR: I hear you, Huss. I really do.

ABE: So come to the hearing next Thursday.

AMIR: Next Thursday's a busy day at work.

ABE: An old man who didn't do anything wrong is in prison.

AMIR *(Rough)*: And there's nothing I can do about it.

EMILY: Honey...

Silence.

ABE: I should probably head out.

AMIR: I didn't mean to snap at you...

ABE: Just think about it?

AMIR: Okay. Fine.

Abe hugs his uncle...

EMILY: You okay, sweetie?

ABE: Yeah. Fine.

I really should go.
(With a kiss)
Bye.

EMILY: Bye.

He leaves.

Once he's gone...

AMIR: It will never cease to amaze me. My parents move to this country with my sister, never make her a citizen. When she's old enough? They send her back, marry her off in Pakistan. She has kids with the guy, and lo and behold—he wants to come here. And what do they do? Spend all their spare time at an Islamic center.

EMILY: His heart's in the right place, Amir.

AMIR: Okay. I know.

EMILY: Is yours?

AMIR: What is that supposed to mean?

EMILY *(Coming right in)*: I mean, why would you have worked in the public defender's if you didn't care about justice?

AMIR: Public defenders have the hottest girlfriends.

EMILY: I'd like to think there was some part of you that *believed* in what you were doing. I mean, I don't know...

AMIR: No... Of course.

EMILY: But when it comes to the imam, it's like you don't care. Like you don't think he's human.

AMIR: You and Hussein wanted me to see him? So I went.
I went to talk to him in prison. And the man spent an hour trying to get me to pray again. He's been in prison four months and all he can do—

EMILY *(Cutting him off)*: You told me. So what? So a man who has nothing left but his dignity and his faith is still trying to be useful in the only way he knows how?

I mean, if he feels he needs one of his own people around him—

AMIR: I'm not one of his own people.

EMILY: You are. And in a way that's unique. And that can be helpful to him. Why can't you see that?

AMIR: Can we stop talking about this?

EMILY: We never talk about this. Not really.

Silence.

Amir stares at his wife for a long moment. Something stirring.

EMILY (CONT'D): Amir. I love you.

Lights Out.

Scene Two

Two weeks later.

Emily sits at the dining table. With a cup of morning coffee, the day's paper open before her.

Amir stands opposite her.

EMILY *(Reading)*: "The defendant, surrounded by a gauntlet of attorneys, struck a defiant tone. He spoke eloquently of the injustices he'd experienced, and what he called an 'unconscionable lack of due process.' Amir Kapoor of Leibowitz, Bernstein, Harris supported the imam, stating, 'As far as anybody knows, there isn't a case. And if the Justice Department has one, it's time they started making it.'"
(Beat)
    I don't think you look like counsel for the defense.
AMIR: That's because you know I'm not.
EMILY: It's because it doesn't say you are.
AMIR *(Taking the paper)*: "The defendant, surrounded by a gauntlet of attorneys, struck a defiant tone." And then she quotes an attorney. Me. Implying that I'm one of the gauntlet of attorneys. She doesn't quote another attorney.
EMILY: But she says you're just supporting him.

AMIR: I don't see a *just*. There's no *just supporting him*.

EMILY: It's implied.

AMIR: I think it reads very clearly that I was supporting his defiant tone. That I was supporting him being defiant.

EMILY: Isn't he justified?

AMIR: That's not my point, Em.

EMILY: Maybe it should be.

AMIR: The man's basically an alleged terrorist.
 (Off another look at the paper)
  Amir Kapoor supported the imam...

EMILY: Even if it does make you look—

AMIR *(Leaping in)*: So it does?

EMILY: I don't think it does. But even *if* it does, why is that a bad
thing? What you did is right. You're standing up for due
process.

AMIR: It's just...

EMILY: What?

AMIR: Don't you think people are going to think...
 (Beat)
  I guess they'll look at the name; if they know anything at all—

EMILY *(Over)*: Amir.

AMIR: —they'll know the name isn't Muslim.

Beat.

EMILY: Amir. What's going on?
 (Beat)
  If this bothers you so much, call the *Times*. Have them
retract.

AMIR: But the thing is, I did say this.

EMILY *(Proudly)*: I remember.

AMIR: But after clearly saying I was *not* counsel for the defendant.
(Beat)
> Why did they have to mention the firm?

Pause.

EMILY: Baby.
> You did the right thing. I am so proud of you. So was Abe. And you'll see. Mort's gonna be proud of you, too.
AMIR: Mort's not the one I'm worried about.
EMILY: This is going to be good for you at work.
AMIR: Good for me?
EMILY: Look at Goldman.
AMIR: Goldman?
EMILY: Sachs
> Jamie? He took all that philanthropy so seriously...
AMIR: What does your douche-bag banker ex-boyfriend have to do with this?
EMILY: Isn't that how it works?
> Isn't that how all you guys cover up the fact that all anybody cares about in your world is making money?
AMIR: I have to get going.
(Still caught up by the paper)
> "...supported the imam..."
EMILY: Honey, honey. Look at me. Stop it.

The intercom BUZZES.

Sudden silence.

EMILY (CONT'D): That's Isaac.
AMIR *(Off Emily's shift)*: Yeah?

EMILY: Well, I mean he's here.

AMIR: Okay.

EMILY: What?

AMIR *(Disgusted)*: Nothing.

EMILY: Do you want to keep talking about this?

AMIR: I need to go.

EMILY: Are you annoyed with me?

(Beat)

Honey, this is a big deal. I have a studio visit with a curator from the Whitney.

AMIR: And who do you think made it happen?

EMILY: Really? Now? Can we talk about this tonight?

AMIR *(Curt)*: There's nothing to talk about.

Amir exits to the bedroom.

Emily goes to the intercom.

EMILY: Hi. Yes. Send him up.

(To Amir, off stage)

I mean, I'm sure no one'll see it. It's buried in the back...

AMIR *(Returning)*: Don't.

EMILY: Don't what?

AMIR: I know your mind is elsewhere.

EMILY: I just...I think you're overthinking this.

AMIR: Let me get this straight: Some waiter is a dick to me in a restaurant and you want to make a painting. But if it's something that actually might affect my livelihood, you don't even want to believe there could be a problem.

EMILY: What does one thing have to do with the other?

KNOCKING at the door.

Beat. Tense standoff.

Amir checks his pockets.

AMIR: I left my phone in the bedroom.

He exits again.

Emily gathers herself as she heads to the door...

And opens it to show...

ISAAC—40, white, smart, attractive. A curator at the Whitney.

ISAAC: Hi.
EMILY: Hi. How are you?
ISAAC: Great.
EMILY: Find it okay?
ISAAC: Quick ride up Madison. Couldn't be easier.

We hear SOUNDS offstage of Amir slamming around in the bedroom. Looking for his phone.

EMILY: Amir's on his way out...

Amir reenters.

The tension between him and Emily still palpable.

AMIR: Isaac.

ISAAC: Hello, sir.

AMIR: Good to see you.

(Beat)

Thanks again for a wonderful weekend in the country.

ISAAC: Was our pleasure.

AMIR: I—uh—gotta run. I'm late for work.

ISAAC: You'll probably still get there before my wife.

AMIR: Always do.

(To Emily, coldly)

See you later.

EMILY: Bye, honey.

(To Amir, intimately)

It's gonna be fine. You'll see.

Amir exits.

Beat.

ISAAC: Is this a bad time?

EMILY: No. No.

ISAAC: You sure?

EMILY: Yeah.

ISAAC: I mean—okay.

EMILY: Can I get you some coffee, tea?

ISAAC: Sure. Coffee'd be great.

EMILY: Milk? Sugar?

ISAAC: Black is fine.

Emily heads for the kitchen.

Leaving Isaac onstage. He takes a look around. Perhaps just a hint intrusively.

He picks up a book off the shelf.

Emily returns with a mug.

ISAAC (CONT'D): Constable's great, isn't he?

EMILY: Love him.

ISAAC: It's one of the things I love about going to Frieze every
year. My little pilgrimage to see the Constables at the Tate.
(Putting the book back)
You ever been?

EMILY: Tate, yes.
Frieze, no. Though my dealer suggested I go this year.

Isaac takes the mug.

ISAAC: Thanks.
So I've spent a lot of time thinking about our discussions
since last weekend.

EMILY: About me being a white woman with no right to be using
Islamic forms?
I think you're wrong about that.

ISAAC: I think I might be wrong, too.

Beat.

EMILY: What happened?

ISAAC: Well, I found a few images of your work online...

EMILY: You read Jerry's review.

ISAAC: Yes, I did.
I don't always agree with Jerry. But he did have some
compelling things to say...
(Turning to the painting above the mantel)
This is the one you wanted me to see?

EMILY: This is the one in the apartment.
There are more at the studio.

Isaac inspects the paintings for a long beat.

ISAAC: Mm-hmm...
I have to admit...
It has presence...
(Stepping back, assessing)
The surface tending toward the convex...
It's a bending of the picture plane, isn't it?
EMILY: Exactly.
ISAAC: Which is why Jerry was talking about late Bonnard.
EMILY: The mosaics in Andalusia are bending the picture plane four hundred years before Bonnard. That's what I mean. That's what I was saying. The Muslims gave us Aristotle. Without them, we probably wouldn't even have visual perspective.
ISAAC: That's quite a statement.
EMILY: And I can back it up.
(Beat, then off Isaac's reaction)
What?
ISAAC: I don't know...
It's the earnestness. The lack of irony. It's unusual...
EMILY: Irony's overrated.
ISAAC: Can't say I disagree with that.
EMILY: But?
ISAAC: You know what you're going to be accused of...
(Off Emily's silence)
Orientalism...

I mean, hell. You've even got the brown husband.

EMILY: Fuck you, I think.

Beat.

ISAAC: Good.

Because that's what they're going to say.

Beat.

EMILY: Yeah. Well, we've all gotten way too wrapped up in the optics. The way we talk about things. We've forgotten to look at things for what they really are.

(Beat)

When you're at Frieze this fall, after the Constables, you need to go to the Victoria and Albert. The Islamic galleries. Room forty-two. Remember that. It will change the way you see art.

ISAAC *(Warmly)*: Them's fightin' words.

Beat.

EMILY: The Islamic tiling tradition, Isaac? Is a doorway to the most extraordinary freedom. And which only comes through a kind of profound submission. In my case, of course it's not submission to Islam but to the formal language. The pattern. The repetition. And the quiet that this work requires of me? It's extraordinary.

ISAAC: You sound like a midcentury American minimalist, trying to obliterate the ego.

EMILY: The Islamic tradition's been doing it for a thousand years. Pardon me for thinking they may have a better handle on it.

(Beat)

It's time we woke up. Time we stop paying lip service to Islam and Islamic art. We draw on the Greeks, the Romans... but Islam is part of who we are, too. God forbid anybody remind us of it.

ISAAC: Huh.

EMILY: What?

ISAAC: No, this is good.

EMILY: Yeah.

Lights Out.

Scene Three

Three months later.

Lights come up. On the terrace, Amir. A drink in hand.

He drinks. Drinks again. Stares down into the bottom of his glass. Burning.

Beat.

Then all at once, he SMASHES the glass on the terrace floor. Shards fly.

Beat.

The burst of violence doesn't seem to have soothed him. He comes into the apartment. Going to the bar for a glass, and another drink.

Finally, we hear—KEYS...

The door opens and Emily enters with grocery bags.

EMILY: Hey, honey.
AMIR: Hey.
      Where were you?
EMILY: At Gourmet Garage. Getting a few things. For tonight.
AMIR: Tonight?

EMILY: Isaac and Jory. You didn't forget, did you?

AMIR: That's why it smells so good in here.

EMILY: I made pork tenderloin. And guess what…

(Pulling something from the bag)

…they had La Tur! And that liver mousse you love so much.

AMIR: Great.

EMILY: Can't be bad news, right? "I'm coming to your house to eat your food and tell you you're not in the show." Nobody does that, right?

AMIR: So you're in.

EMILY: God, I hope.

Emily approaching him. Sexual.

AMIR: Honey.

EMILY: What?

AMIR: We've talked about this.

(Beat)

It doesn't help.

EMILY: I miss you, Amir.

AMIR: I know.

Beat.

EMILY: So I'm assuming you forgot the wine.

AMIR: I did. I'm sorry.

EMILY: Amir.

AMIR: I said I'm sorry.

Beat.

EMILY: What's wrong?

AMIR: Nothing.

EMILY: Something's wrong.

Pause.

AMIR: I had a meeting with a couple of the partners today. I mean, if you could call it that. I'm in my office, red-lining a contract due at six. Steven comes in. With Jack. Sits down. Asks me where my parents were born.

EMILY: Pakistan.

AMIR: I said India.

That's what I put on the form when I got hired.

EMILY: Why?

AMIR: It technically *was* India when my dad was born.

EMILY: Okay.

AMIR: *But the names of the cities you've listed are not in India,* Steven says. *They're in Pakistan.*

My father was born in 1946. When it was all one country, before the British chopped it up into two countries in 1947.

And your mother was born when?

1948.

So it wasn't India anymore, was it? It was Pakistan?

My clock is running, and I'm wasting time on a fucking history lesson.

Turns out, Steven's trying to ascertain if I misrepresented myself.

EMILY: It sounds like you did.

AMIR: It was all India. So there's a different name on it now. So what?

(Beat)

　　He knew about my name change. *Your birth name is not Kapoor,* Steven says. *It's Abdullah. Why did you change it?*

EMILY: Didn't he already know?

AMIR: I never told them.

EMILY: They must have run a background check.

AMIR: I—uh—had my Social Security number changed. When I changed my name.

EMILY: You did?

AMIR: Yeah. It was before I met you.

EMILY: Is that legal?

AMIR: They do it all the time. When people go through identity theft.

　　Steven must have been digging around. He has it in for me. I knew I never should have gone to that hearing.

EMILY: That was months ago. What does that have to do with anything?

AMIR: A lot, honey. A lot.

Beat.

EMILY: Have you talked to Mort about it?

AMIR: I can't get ahold of him.

The intercom BUZZES.

EMILY: Wait a second. What time is it?

AMIR *(Checking his watch)*: Ten past.

EMILY: What're they doing here?

　　I still have to get ready.

AMIR: Go get ready. I'll get it.

Amir heads for the kitchen.

AMIR (CONT'D) *(At the intercom, off stage)*: Yes?
    Send them up.
EMILY *(As Amir reemerges)*: You gonna be okay?
AMIR: I'll be fine.
EMILY: You sure?
AMIR: Yes. Go.
EMILY: Can you get the appetizers? They're on the counter in the
    kitchen.
AMIR: I got it.

Emily exits.

*Amir goes to the door. Turning the bolt to prop the door.
Then takes the bags into the kitchen.*

*We hear NOISES outside the door. Then the door creeps
open.*

WOMAN'S VOICE: Amir?

Just as Amir emerges—

AMIR: Come on in, Jor.

Enter:

*Jory—mid- to late 30s, African American—is command-
ing, forthright, intelligent. Almost masculine.*

We've seen Isaac before.

Both shed their coats as Amir gets to them.

ISAAC *(Shaking hands)*: Good to see you again.

AMIR: Good to see you, too.

JORY: Hey, Amir.

AMIR: Hi, Jory.

Did we say seven thirty?

ISAAC: I was sure she said seven.

JORY *(To Isaac)*: I told you.

AMIR: She's still getting ready.

JORY: No worries.

AMIR: More time to drink, right?

JORY *(Showing a box)*: We brought dessert.

AMIR: Magnolia Bakery? Thank you.

JORY *(Heading off)*: This should go in the fridge.

ISAAC *(To Amir)*: I was at the Knicks game last night.

AMIR: You were?

ISAAC: Aren't you a Knicks fan?

AMIR: I'm sorry to say.

ISAAC: No dishonor in it.

AMIR: No dishonor. But lots of pain.

ISAAC: I'm a Cubs fan. Don't get me started on pain.

Jory returns to hear:

AMIR: Oh, the Bartman.

ISAAC: I mean, I didn't think he should be killed.

But I had friends...

AMIR: Killed?

JORY: Who's Bartman?

ISAAC: Honey.

AMIR: The fan who stole the ball out of a Cubs outfielder's hand...

ISAAC: Moisés Alou. Eighth inning.

AMIR: And denied the Cubs a trip to the World Series.

ISAAC *(To Jory)*: You don't remember this?

JORY: It's ringing a bell.

> *(Beat)*
>
> Smells great in here.

AMIR: Em's making pork tenderloin.

> *(To Isaac)*
>
> You eat pork, don't you?

JORY: Every chance he gets...

ISAAC: Gotta make up for all the lost years...

> Could I use your restroom?

AMIR: Down the hall on the right.

ISAAC: I remember.

> *Isaac crosses to the hall. Exits.*

AMIR: What are you drinking?

JORY: You have scotch?

AMIR: Still have that bottle of Macallan that you gave me.

JORY: I expect more from you, Amir.

AMIR: We'll finish it tonight.

> On the rocks?

JORY: Neat.

AMIR: You're not kidding around.

> *Amir begins to prepare the drink...*

JORY: You hear about Sarah?

AMIR: What about her?

JORY: She got her terrier back.

AMIR: How?

JORY: She hired a dog investigator who kidnapped it back from Frank.

AMIR: Lord.

JORY: Frank's gonna sue her.

AMIR: On what grounds?

JORY: Just to make her life miserable.

AMIR: The two of them.

JORY: Tell me about it.

>*(Taking a drink from Amir)*
>
>She and I ran into Frank at the courthouse.

AMIR: Oh, you were in court today?

JORY: Proctor insurance arbitration.

AMIR: How'd it go?

JORY: Fine. We're just dancing around the number now. They have to pay and they know it. They just need a little time to get used to the idea.

AMIR: Mort there?

JORY: Steven took it over. He has me on it now.

AMIR: But Proctor's Mort's.

JORY: Was.

AMIR: Why is that not a surprise?

JORY: Mort couldn't be bothered. Rather be meditating.

AMIR: Yeah, instead of taking his Lipitor.

JORY: You know he took me to lunch and tried to teach me to meditate? I actually tried it a couple of times. Ended up gaining five pounds. I just kept thinking about food. I'd get frustrated, give up, and pig out.

AMIR: What's up with the offer from Credit Suisse?

JORY: I'm not gonna do it.

AMIR: Didn't they come back with two hundred more?

JORY: They did.

AMIR: I told you that move would work.

JORY: You were right.

AMIR: But I don't think you can get more...

Beat.

JORY: The partners are countering.

AMIR: I doubt it's two hundred more.

JORY: I've put down roots.

Beat.

AMIR: Kapoor, Brathwaite.

JORY: What?

AMIR: You and me. On our own. In business.
    Steven and Mort got ahead underpricing the competition.
    Back in the day, when they got started.

JORY: Well, downtown WASPs didn't want to be doing mergers
    and acquisitions.

AMIR: Yeah, fine. That's why Jews were doing it. And then merg-
    ers and acquisitions became all the rage. And guys like
    Steven and Mort became the establishment.
    We are the new Jews.

JORY: Okay...

AMIR: We go about it the right way? We'll get to where LBH is
    now in a quarter of the time it took them.

JORY: You coming up with this on the fly?

AMIR: This afternoon.
    That firm will never be ours. It's theirs. And they're always
    going to remind us that we were just invited to the party.

JORY: I don't think it's a bad idea.

AYAD AKHTAR

> *(Beat)*
> Amir—
>
> *Just as...*
>
> *...Isaac returns from the bathroom, holding a book.*

ISAAC: Who's reading this?
> ...Sorry, am I interrupting?

JORY: Well...

AMIR: Just talking shop.

> *Just as Emily enters, looking lovely.*

EMILY: I'm so sorry.
> *(To Jory)*
> Nice to see you.

JORY: Nice to see you, too.

ISAAC: Hey, Em.

EMILY: Hi, Isaac.

ISAAC: I'm sorry, I thought I heard seven.

EMILY: Look. As long as you don't mind waiting for dinner...

AMIR: Honey, they got cupcakes from Magnolia.

JORY: Banana pudding, actually.

EMILY: Oh, my God. I love that stuff.

JORY: It's like crack.

AMIR: You want something to drink, Isaac?

ISAAC: Scotch'd be great. On the rocks...

AMIR: Honey?

EMILY: Port.

JORY: Port? Before dinner?

EMILY: I know I'm strange. I just love it so much...

Amir gets started on the drinks.

ISAAC *(To Emily)*: So who's reading *Denial of Death*?

EMILY: I am. Since you suggested it.

AMIR *(To Isaac)*: She's been raving about it.

ISAAC: The only reason people remember this anymore is because it's the book Woody Allen gives to Diane Keaton on their first date in *Annie Hall*. And tells her: "This is everything you need to know about me."

AMIR: Denial of death.

JORY *(To Isaac)*: You should've given me a heads-up, too.

ISAAC: You think?

It's an amazing book. I actually got the title for my new show from here...

AMIR: What's the title?

Amir hands out drinks.

ISAAC: The title... Well, first let me say —

It's been generations and generations of consumerism and cynicism.

JORY *(Over)*: Get comfortable.

ISAAC *(Continuing)*: ...And an art market that just feeds the frenzy. But something's shifting. There's a movement of young artists who are not buying into it anymore.

They're asking the question — how to make art sacred again. It's an impossibly heroic task they've set for themselves. Which is why I'm calling it...

(Gesturing to Jory to hold her criticism)

Impossible Heroes.

(Off Jory's reaction)
    She doesn't like it.

JORY: It sounds like a segment on Anderson Cooper's *360.*

AMIR: About Paralympic athletes.

JORY: The impossible heroes.

ISAAC: Very funny.
    How about you, Em? What do you think of the title?
    After all, it's your show now, too...

Beat.

EMILY: You're kidding?

ISAAC: The work you're doing with the Islamic tradition is
    important and new. It needs to be seen. Widely.

EMILY: Isaac, that's amazing. Thank you. Thank you so much.

Ensuing congratulations overlap...

JORY: Congratulations, Emily.

EMILY: Thank you.

AMIR: That's incredible. I'm so proud of you, honey.

ISAAC *(Lifting his glass)*: A toast is in order. To—

AMIR *(Over)*: To your show. And to Emily in your show.

ALL: Cheers...

All drink.

AMIR: So...how many?

ISAAC: What?

AMIR: Of her paintings?

EMILY: That's my husband. Always talking numbers.

ISAAC: I've got room for four or five.

AMIR: Five. That sounds great.

Laughter.

ISAAC *(Pointing to the canvas above the fireplace)*: I definitely want *that* one. The couple I saw in the studio. And I've been thinking about the *Study After Velázquez's Moor.* But I'm not sure...

JORY: Moor?

Haven't heard that word in a minute.

EMILY: I did a portrait of Amir a few months ago...

After an episode we had at a...

Noticing Amir's reaction to her bringing up the story, Emily shifts gears...

EMILY (CONT'D): I'd just been to the Met and seen the Velázquez painting.

Emily goes to the bookshelf in the corner.

JORY: Which one?

EMILY: *Portrait of Juan de Pareja*—who happened to be of Moorish descent.

(Returning with the book)

This is the original portrait.

JORY *(Recognizing)*: Oh. Of course.

EMILY: It's a study after the Velázquez. I'm using the same palette, same composition. But it's a portrait of Amir.

AMIR: Your very own personal Moor.

EMILY: *Muse* is more like it...

ISAAC: I think I'd rather stick with the abstract pieces. Keep the impression of your work consolidated. But I'm tempted. I mean, it's a stunning portrait. Quite a tribute to you, Amir, if you ask me...

AMIR: You think?

ISAAC: Standing there in your black suit. Silver cuff links. Perfectly pressed lily-white dress shirt...

(To Emily)

...which is so magnificently rendered. You can almost smell the starch on that shirt.

AMIR: Not starch, Isaac. Just ridiculous thread count.

JORY: People do not stop talking about your shirts at the office.

AMIR: Really?

JORY: Sarah was joking you must spend half what you make on shirts.

EMILY: Wouldn't be far from the truth. Charvet, always.

JORY: How much do those run?

Amir seems reluctant to reply.

EMILY: Six hundred.

JORY: Dollars?

ISAAC: So there you are, in your six-hundred-dollar Charvet shirt, like Velázquez's brilliant apprentice-slave in his lace collar, adorned in the splendors of the world you're now so clearly a part of...

And yet...

AMIR: Yeah?

ISAAC: The question remains.

AMIR: The question?

ISAAC: Of your place.

For the viewer, of course. Not you.

It's a painting, after all...

Pause.

AMIR: I like the stuff she was doing before.

ISAAC: The landscapes? Not a huge fan.

JORY: Isaac.

ISAAC: What? She knows that. I think it's smart she moved on. It's not as fertile a direction for her.

AMIR: I think the landscapes are very *fertile.*

EMILY: Amir...

AMIR: What?

EMILY: We both know why you like the landscapes.

JORY: Why?

EMILY: Because they have nothing to do with Islam.

ISAAC *(Before Amir can speak)*: What she's doing with the Islamic tradition has taken her to another level.

A young Western painter drawing on Islamic representation? Not *ironically?* But in *service?*

It's an unusual and remarkable statement.

AMIR: What's the statement?

ISAAC: Islam is rich and universal. Part of a spiritual and artistic heritage we can all draw from.

(To Emily)

I loved that thing you said in London. At the Frieze Art Fair. About humility and the Renaissance...

EMILY: Right. The Renaissance is when we turned away from something bigger than ourselves. It put the individual at the center of the universe and made a cult out of the personal ego.

ISAAC: Right.

EMILY: That never happened in the Islamic tradition. It's still more connected to a wider, less personal perspective.

ISAAC: I'm using that in the catalogue.

EMILY: Stop it.

ISAAC: I'm serious. You've got a major career ahead of you.
I'm just one of the first to get to the party.
Emily Hughes-Kapoor. A name to be contended with.

AMIR: Hear, hear.

Toasting...

JORY: Kapoor.
Where in India is that name from?

Pause.

AMIR: Why are you asking?

JORY: Did I say something wrong?

AMIR: No, no...
Steven came into my office today and asked me the same thing.

JORY: He did?

Awkward pause.

EMILY: You know—it's a pretty common Punjabi name.

ISAAC: I'm headed to Delhi day after tomorrow. That's in Punjab, isn't it?

AMIR: Not really, but...Same country...So...Why not?

Laughs.

EMILY: What are you doing in Delhi, Isaac?

ISAAC: Sothi Sikander has deigned to offer me a studio visit.

EMILY: How exciting. I love his work.
(To Jory)
You going, too?

JORY: Ezra has school.

ISAAC: Jory's being polite. It's not because Ezra has school. I have a...little bit of an issue when it comes to flying.

JORY: That's one way of putting it.

ISAAC: I hate flying.

It's a primal thing.

The thought of not being on the ground...opens up this door to like every fear I have—and the hysteria around security only makes it worse.

AMIR: It's a nightmare at the airports.

JORY: And now there's a whole new attraction. You get to decide between being ogled over or felt up.

ISAAC: Felt up. Definitely.

JORY: Why is that not a surprise?

ISAAC: It actually calms me down.

(To Amir)

What's that like for you?

AMIR: What?

ISAAC: Security at airports.

(Awkward beat)

I mean, you hear stories...

AMIR: Wouldn't know. I cut right to the chase.

EMILY: He volunteers himself. Goes right to the agents and offers himself up.

JORY: What? To be searched?

AMIR: I know they're looking at me. And it's not because I look like Giselle. I figure why not make it easier for everyone involved...

JORY: Never heard of anyone doing *that* before...

AMIR: On top of people being more and more *afraid* of folks who look like me, we end up being *resented*, too.

EMILY: Those agents are working hard *not* to discriminate...
Then here's this guy who comes up to them and calls them out...

AMIR: Pure, unmitigated passive aggression. That's what my wife thinks.

ISAAC: Maybe she's got a point.

JORY: I think it's kind of admirable, Amir. If everyone was so forthcoming, the world would be a very different place.

ISAAC: It's racial profiling.

JORY: Honey. I know what it is.

ISAAC: I can't imagine you'd like that if it was you?

AMIR: It's not her. That's the point.

JORY: ...And it's probably not some Kansas grandmother in a wheelchair.

AMIR: The next terrorist attack is probably gonna come from some guy who more or less looks like me.

EMILY: I totally disagree. The next attack is coming from some white guy who's got a gun he shouldn't have...

AMIR: And pointing it at a guy who looks like me.

EMILY: Not necessarily.

ISAAC *(To Amir)*: If every person of Middle Eastern descent started doing what you're doing...

AMIR: Yeah?

ISAAC: I mean, if we all got used to that kind of...*compliance?*
We might actually start getting a little too comfortable about our suspicions...

AMIR: So you do have suspicions?

ISAAC: I mean, not *me*, I'm just saying—

AMIR: Look. Hell. I don't blame you.

ISAAC: Wait. What?

EMILY *(To Amir, abruptly)*: Could you get me a glass of port?

> Emily hands Amir her glass. As...

> Her cell phone RINGS—on the coffee table.

> Emily checks it. Without answering.

EMILY *(To Amir)*: It's Abe.

AMIR: Abe?

EMILY: Your nephew?

AMIR: What's he calling you about?

EMILY: Did he call you and you not call him back?

AMIR: Yeah.

EMILY: So he's calling me.
>> You gotta work on that, honey.
>> *(To Jory and Isaac)*
>> You guys hungry?

JORY: Getting there.

EMILY *(Getting up)*: I'm starting us with a fennel salad.
>> *(To Jory)*
>> You eat anchovies?

JORY: Love them. And I *love* fennel.

AMIR *(Pouring a drink)*: Her fennel-anchovy salad is a classic. A fucking classic.

JORY *(To Isaac, but indicating Amir)*: See, honey.
>> An exemplary instance of spousal support. He never compliments me on my cooking.

ISAAC: I do most of the cooking.

JORY: Because you don't show me any love when I do.

ISAAC: Look. You make a good omelet.

JORY: I haven't made an omelet in ages.

ISAAC: Might be the best thing about them.

EMILY *(Getting up, for the kitchen)*: I can't believe you just said that.

JORY *(To Emily)*: Would you like some help?

EMILY: Thank you, Jory. I would love some.

ISAAC: Just keep her away from the ingredients.

Emily and Jory exit.

ISAAC (CONT'D) *(To Amir)*: So...

I'm sorry if I brought up something sensitive...

Between you and Emily, I mean...

AMIR: You didn't.

ISAAC: Oh.

AMIR: It's not a secret. Em and I don't see eye to eye on Islam. I think it's...a backward way of thinking. And being.

ISAAC: You don't think that's maybe a little broad?

I mean, it happens to be one of the world's great spiritual traditions.

AMIR: Let me guess. You're reading Rumi.

ISAAC: Amir...

Actually. Yes, I've been reading Rumi. And he's great. But that's not what I'm talking about.

Do you know Hanif Saeed?

AMIR: I don't.

ISAAC: He's a sculptor, he's Muslim, he's devout. His work is an amazing testimony to the power of faith. He carves these monolithic pillar-like forms—

AMIR *(Interrupting)*: Have you read the Quran, Isaac?

ISAAC: I haven't.

AMIR: When it comes to Islam? Monolithic pillar-like forms don't matter...

Just as Emily and Jory return with the salad and bowls...

AMIR (CONT'D): And paintings don't matter. Only the Quran matters.

EMILY: Paintings don't matter?

AMIR: I didn't mean it like that.

EMILY: How did you mean it?

AMIR: Honey. You're aware of what the Prophet said about them?

EMILY: I am, Amir.

JORY: What did he say?

AMIR: He used to say angels don't enter a house where there are pictures and/or dogs.

JORY: What's wrong with dogs?

AMIR: Your guess is as good as mine.

ISAAC: Every religion's got idiosyncrasies. My ancestors didn't like lobster. Who doesn't like lobster? What's your point?

AMIR: My point is that what a few artists are doing, however wonderful, does not reflect the Muslim psyche.

ISAAC: *Muslim psyche?*

AMIR: Islam comes from the desert.

From a group of tough-minded, tough-living people.

Who saw life as something hard and relentless.

Something to be suffered...

JORY: Huh...

ISAAC: Not the only people to have suffered in a desert for centuries, Amir. Don't know what it says about the *Jewish* psyche, if that's the word we're going to use.

AMIR: Desert pain. I can work with that.

  Jews reacted to the situation differently.

  They turned it over, and over, and over...

  I mean, look at the Talmud. They're looking at things from a hundred different angles, trying to negotiate with it, make it easier, more livable...

JORY: Find new ways to complain about it...

Jory chuckles.

Isaac shoots her a look.

AMIR: Whatever they do, it's not what Muslims do.

  Muslims *don't* think about it. They submit.

  That's what Islam means, by the way. Submission.

ISAAC: I know what it means.

  Look, the problem isn't Islam. It's *Islamo-fascism.*

EMILY: Guys? Salad?

AMIR: Martin Amis, right?

ISAAC: Hitchens, too. They're not wrong about that...

JORY *(Under)*: I'm starving.

AMIR: You haven't read the Quran, but you've read a couple of sanctimonious British bullies and you think you know something about Islam?

Everyone is moving to the table...

EMILY: Amir...

AMIR: What? That's not fair game? If he's going to offer it as a counter, it's fair game.

ISAAC: He has a point. I need to read the Koran.

EMILY *(To Isaac)*: Did you want fresh pepper?

JORY: I had to read some of it in college. All I remember is the anger.

AMIR: Thank you. It's like one very long hate-mail letter to humanity.

EMILY: That's not true!

(With the pepper)

Jory?

AMIR: It is *kind of.* Grant me *that* at least...

EMILY: I'll grant you that the Quran sees humanity as stubborn and self interested—and it takes us to task for that. And I can't say it's wrong to do so—

ISAAC: All I was trying to say with Islamo-fascism is that there's a difference between the religion and the political use of it.

AMIR: Isaac. In Islam there's no difference. There's no distinction between church and state.

JORY: Don't you mean mosque and state?

AMIR: I do. Thank you.

I'm assuming we're all opposed to people who think the Bible is the Constitution?

Last person has been served. All begin to eat.

EMILY: *Bon appétit.*

ISAAC: *Bon appétit.*

JORY: Mmm. This is so good.

AMIR: Did I tell you, or did I tell you?

EMILY: It's so easy. You slice everything up...

ISAAC *(Looking at his plate)*: Fennel, peppers, celery...

EMILY: ...carrots, radishes...

ISAAC: What are these?

EMILY: Baby artichokes...

JORY *(Coming in)*: What gets me just as much as people who treat the Bible like the Constitution are the people who treat the Constitution like it's the Bible. I mean, trying to figure out what a text written more than two hundred years ago really meant? Like it's going to solve our problems today?

EMILY: Like all that bullshit about the right to bear arms. It was 1791, people.

AMIR: That's my point. That's exactly what I'm saying. Honey.

ISAAC: Mmm. This is delicious, Em. Really.

EMILY: I picked up the recipe when I was on a Fulbright in Seville.

ISAAC: I love Spain. I ran with the bulls in Pamplona.

JORY: You did not run with the bulls.

ISAAC: I watched people run with the bulls. It was thrilling.

AMIR: We went to Barcelona for our honeymoon.

The chorizo. The paella. The wine.

Spanish wines are so underrated.

ISAAC: See, this is the problem I'm having...

You're saying Muslims are so different. *You're* not that different.

You have the same idea of *the good life* as I do. I wouldn't have even known you were a Muslim if it wasn't for the article in the *Times*.

Pause.

AMIR: I'm not Muslim. I'm an *apostate*. Which means I've renounced my faith.

ISAAC *(Overlapping)*: I know what the word *apostate* means.

JORY: Isaac?

AMIR: Do you also know that—according to the Quran—it makes me punishable by death?

EMILY: That's not true, Amir.

AMIR: Yes, it is.

EMILY: Have you even read that part?

Have you?

It condemns renouncing the faith, but it doesn't specify punishment. The tradition has *interpreted* it as punishable by death.

JORY: Impressive...

EMILY: He's repeated it enough, I checked. I have a vested interest, after all.

Women laugh.

AMIR: Fine.

So let's talk about something that *is* in the text.

Wife beating.

ISAAC: Wife beating?

JORY: Great. Could you pass the bread?

EMILY: Amir, really?

AMIR *(Passing the bread)*: So the angel Gabriel comes to Muhammad...

ISAAC: Angel Gabriel?

AMIR *(Mocking)*: Yeah. That's how Muslims believe the Quran came to humanity. The angel Gabriel supposedly dictated it to Muhammad word for word.

ISAAC: Like Joseph Smith. Mormonism.

An angel named Marami came down in upstate New York and talked to Joseph Smith—

JORY: Moroni, honey. Not Marami.

ISAAC: You sure?

JORY: It was on *South Park*.

Beat.

AMIR: So like I was saying...

The angel Gabriel shows up and teaches Muhammad this verse. You know the one, honey.

I'm paraphrasing...

Men are in charge of women...

EMILY: Amir?

AMIR *(Continuing)*:

If they don't obey...

Talk to them.

If that doesn't work...

Don't sleep with them.

And if that doesn't work...

(Turning to Emily)

Em?

EMILY: I'm not doing this.

AMIR: *Beat them.*

JORY: I don't remember that being in the Koran.

AMIR: Oh, it's there all right.

EMILY: The usual translation is debatable.

AMIR: Only for people who are trying to make Islam look all warm and fuzzy.

EMILY: The root verb can mean beat. But it can also mean leave. So it could be saying, if your wife doesn't listen, leave her. Not beat her.

ISAAC: Sounds like a pretty big difference.

AMIR: That's not how it's been interpreted for hundreds of years.

JORY *(Suddenly impassioned)*: No. See. Sometimes you just have to say no.

I don't blame the French.

ISAAC: The French?

JORY: For their problem with Islam.

ISAAC: You're okay with them banning the veil?

JORY: You do have to draw the line *somewhere*.

ISAAC: Okay, Mrs. Kissinger.

EMILY: Endearing.

ISAAC: I'm married to a woman who has a Kissinger quote above her desk in the den...

JORY: *"If faced with choosing justice or order, I'll always choose order."*

EMILY: Why do you have that above your desk?

JORY: To remind me. Not to get lost in the feeling that I need to get *justice*.

You pull yourself out of the ghetto, you realize *real soon* order is where it's at...

EMILY: Me. Justice. Always.

JORY: You know what they say? If you're young and not a liberal, you've got no heart. And if you're old and not a conservative...

AMIR AND JORY *(Together)*: ...you've got no brain.

ISAAC: I happen to know a few very brilliant Muslim women who *choose* to wear the veil.

AMIR: You really enjoy playing the contrarian, don't you?

ISAAC: I'm not playing the contrarian.

JORY *(To Isaac, over)*: Who do you know that wears the veil?

ISAAC: You wouldn't know them.

JORY: I think you're making it up.

ISAAC: I'm not.

JORY: So who?

ISAAC: Khalid's sister.

JORY: Khalid?

ISAAC: She's a professor of philosophy at Cornell.
　　　She wears the veil.

JORY: Khalid? Your trainer?

AMIR: You train at Equinox?

ISAAC: Yeah.

AMIR: I know Khalid. Balding? With the guns?

ISAAC: That's him. I didn't know you trained at Equinox.

JORY: What's your point?

ISAAC: Khalid may be a trainer, but he comes from a ridiculously educated Jordanian background. All the women in his family wear the veil. By choice.

EMILY: It's not always what people think. It's a source of pride for a lot of Muslim women.

AMIR: First of all, they're probably wearing headscarves. Not the veil. It's not the same thing —

JORY *(Cutting in)*: The veil is evil.
　　　You erase a face, you erase individuality.
　　　Nobody's making men erase their individuality.
　　　Why's it always come down to making the woman pay?

Uh-uh. There is a point at which you just have to say no.

AMIR: Just say no.

That is exactly what Muhammad *didn't* do.

Here's the irony:

Before becoming a prophet? He was adamant about his followers *not* abusing women.

And then he starts talking to an angel.

I mean, *really?*

ISAAC: I still can't believe I've never seen the parallel with Mormonism before.

AMIR: You keep saying *that* like it means something.

ISAAC: Both religions where you can have multiple wives, too. Though I think Mormons are okay with dogs.

AMIR: You still don't get it.

ISAAC: Get what? That you're full of self-loathing?

Jory shoots Isaac a look to kill.

AMIR: The Quran is about tribal life in a seventh-century desert, Isaac.

The point isn't just academic.

There's a result to believing that a book written about life in a specific society fifteen hundred years ago is the word of God:

You start wanting to *re-create* that society.

After all, it's the only one in which the Quran makes any literal sense.

That's why you have people like the Taliban. They're trying to re-create the world in the image of the one that's in the Quran.

Amir has since gotten up from the table and is now pouring himself another drink.

EMILY: Honey, I think we get it.

AMIR *(To Emily)*: Actually. I'm pretty sure you don't.

(Continuing, to the others)

Here's the kicker. And this is the real problem:

It goes way deeper than the Taliban.

To be Muslim—*truly*—means not only that you *believe* all this. It means you *fight* for it, too.

Politics follows faith?

No distinction between mosque and state?

Remember all that?

So if the point is that the world in the Quran was a better place than this world, well, then let's go back.

Let's stone adulterers.

Let's cut off the hands of thieves.

Let's kill the unbelievers.

And so, even if you're one of those lapsed Muslims sipping your after-dinner scotch alongside your beautiful white American wife—and watching the news and seeing folks in the Middle East dying for values you were taught were purer—and stricter—and truer...you can't help but feel just a little a bit of pride.

ISAAC: Pride?

AMIR: Yes. Pride.

Beat.

ISAAC: Did you feel pride on September Eleventh?

AMIR *(With hesitation)*: If I'm honest, yes.

EMILY: You don't really mean that, Amir.

AMIR: I was horrified by it, okay? Absolutely horrified.

JORY: Pride about what?

　　　About the towers coming down?

　　　About people getting killed?

AMIR: That we were finally winning.

JORY: *We?*

AMIR: Yeah...I guess I forgot...which *we* I was.

JORY: You're an American...

AMIR: It's tribal, Jor. It is in the bones.

　　　You have no idea how I was brought up.

　　　You have to work *real* hard to root that shit out.

JORY: Well, you need to keep working.

AMIR: I am.

Emily has gotten up to go to Amir.

AMIR (CONT'D): What?

EMILY: That's enough.

　　　(Taking his glass)

　　　I'm gonna make you some coffee.

Emily exits to the kitchen.

Long awkward pause.

AMIR: What?

　　　(To Isaac, conciliatory)

　　　Look...

　　　I'm sure it's not all that different than how you feel about
Israel sometimes...

ISAAC: Excuse me?

AMIR: You're going to tell me you've never felt anything like that—an unexpected *blush* of pride, say...

ISAAC: Blush? I don't feel anything like a blush.

AMIR: When you hear about Israel throwing its military weight around?

ISAAC: I'm critical of Israel. A lot of Jews are.

AMIR: And when you hear Ahmadinejad talk about wiping Israel into the Mediterranean, how do you feel then?

ISAAC: Outraged. Like anybody else.

AMIR: Not everybody's outraged. A lot of folks *like* hearing that.

ISAAC: *You* like hearing that?

AMIR: I said a lot of folks...

Emily appears in the kitchen doorway.

ISAAC: I asked you if *you* like hearing it. Do you like hearing about Israel getting wiped into the ocean?

JORY: Isaac...

ISAAC: No. I want to know...

AMIR: Sometimes? Yes...

EMILY *(With hints of despair)*: Amir. We're supposed to be celebrating.

AMIR *(Ignoring, over)*: And I'm saying it's wrong.

And it comes from somewhere.

And that somewhere is Islam.

ISAAC: No shit it's wrong.

But it doesn't come from Islam.

It comes from *you.*

Islam has no monopoly on fundamentalism. It doesn't come from a text.

AMIR: You don't need to patronize me—

ISAAC: You've been patronizing me this whole conversation.

You don't like organized religion? Fine.

You have a particular antipathy for the one you were born into? Fine.

Maybe you feel a little more strongly about it than most of us because... whatever? Fine.

JORY: Isaac.

ISAAC: But I'm not interested in your *absurd*—and frankly, more than a little terrifying—generalizations...

JORY *(Firm)*: Isaac.

ISAAC: What?

JORY: Stop it.

ISAAC: Okay.

Another tense pause.

AMIR: You're naive.

EMILY: Amir. Could you join me in the kitchen?

Emily exits.

AMIR *(Following her out)*: Naive and well-meaning. And you're on a collision course with history.

Amir crosses to the kitchen and exits.

ISAAC: I'm naive? What a fucking asshole.

JORY: He's the asshole?

ISAAC: Did you hear him?

JORY: What's gotten into you?

ISAAC: Fucking closet jihadist.

JORY: Will you shut up?

ISAAC: I will never understand what you see in this guy.

JORY: Something's off tonight.

> I think maybe he knows.

> *(Off Isaac's look)*

> About me.

ISAAC: How would he?

JORY: He's mentioned Steven a few times...

> I don't know? Maybe Mort told him?

ISAAC: Well. He's going to find out sooner or later.

JORY: I wanted to be the one to tell him.

> I owe him that much.

ISAAC: Then you should have told him when it happened.

JORY: I'm under confidentiality.

ISAAC: Well...

JORY: I think I need to tell him.

The kitchen door flies open, and Amir comes bounding back, heading for the coats.

Emily appears behind him.

AMIR *(Clearly intoxicated)*: You came over here with good news. We should be celebrating. It's Emily's night. I'm gonna go get us some champagne.

> *(Off Emily's reaction)*

> And then we're gonna have a wonderful dinner.

Jory and Isaac share a look.

JORY: I'm gonna come with you. Is that okay?

AMIR: Of course.

Amir puts on his coat.

Jory throws on her coat.

Amir looks at Emily.

AMIR (CONT'D): What?
EMILY: Nothing.

Amir pulls open the door.

Both exit.

Emily turns to Isaac.

EMILY (CONT'D): You think I don't know what you're doing?
ISAAC: What am I doing?
EMILY: Isaac, please.
ISAAC: He's a big boy. He can't handle a little push-back?

Emily heads for the side table to pour herself another drink.

ISAAC (CONT'D): You guys get into an argument before we showed up?
EMILY: Why would we get into an argument?
ISAAC: You're married.
EMILY: I don't have the marriage you do.
(*Beat*)
You could have told me about the show over the phone.
ISAAC: I wanted to tell you face-to-face.
EMILY: This is my home.
Isaac...
London...
Was a mistake...
ISAAC: I don't think you really believe that.

Isaac touches her. She pulls away.

ISAAC (CONT'D): You're in the show now, so that's it?

EMILY: If that's why you're putting me in the show...

ISAAC: Of course not. God.

   The whole idea for the show came from you.

Isaac makes another move toward Emily.

Which she doesn't resist at first. Until she pulls away again.

ISAAC (CONT'D): I had no idea your husband was such a mess.
   And a fucking alcoholic to boot.

EMILY: He's not an alcoholic. He had a bad day at the office.

ISAAC: Oh. So he knows.

EMILY: Knows?

ISAAC: About Jory?

EMILY: What about Jory?

ISAAC: They're making her partner.

EMILY: Wait, what?

ISAAC: They offered her a partnership. Name on the firm.
   Their counter to the offer she got from Credit Suisse.

EMILY: When did this happen?

ISAAC: Last week.

EMILY: Nobody told Amir.

ISAAC: Well, Jory's telling him right now.

EMILY: I don't understand.

ISAAC: There is not a lot to understand. They like her. They don't
   like him.

EMILY: Mort's like his father.

ISAAC: Mort doesn't wear the pants. Steven does.

EMILY: Amir's been there twice as long as she has.

ISAAC: Well...

EMILY: What?

ISAAC: The whole thing with the imam?

That Amir represented?

EMILY: He didn't *represent* him.

ISAAC: That's not what the *Times* said.

EMILY: He went to a hearing.

ISAAC: The paper mentioned the firm and they mentioned Amir and it looked like he was representing a man who was raising money for terrorists.

EMILY: That's absurd.

ISAAC: That's not what Steven thought. He went ballistic.

EMILY: He did?

ISAAC: Don't you know this?

Jory said your husband broke down. Was crying at a staff meeting. And apparently shouted something about how if the imam had been a *rabbi,* Steven wouldn't have cared.

Steven thought the comment was anti-Semitic.

EMILY: I'm sorry, but sometimes you people have a problem.

ISAAC: We people?

EMILY: Jews. You see anti-Semitism everywhere.

ISAAC: You're married to a man who feels a blush when Ahmadinejad talks about wiping Jews into the ocean. Steven is a huge fund-raiser for Netanyahu. I have no idea why Amir would go anywhere near a guy like that imam.

EMILY *(Crushed)*: For me. He did it for me.

Oh, God.

Pause.

ISAAC: He doesn't understand you. He can't understand you.

He puts you on a pedestal.

It's in your painting.

Study After Velázquez.

He's looking out at the viewer—that viewer is you. You painted it. He's looking at you.

The expression on that face?

Shame. Anger. Pride.

Yeah. The pride he was talking about.

The slave finally has the master's wife.

EMILY: You're disgusting—

ISAAC: It's the truth, Em. And you know it. You painted it.

Silence.

ISAAC (CONT'D): If what happened that night in London was a mistake, Em, it's not the last time you're going to make it.

A man like that…

You *will* cheat on him again. Maybe not with me, but you will.

EMILY: Isaac.

ISAAC: And then one day you'll leave him.

Em. I'm in love with you.

Isaac leans in to kiss her.

Emily doesn't move. In or out.

Just as the front door opens—

Jory enters. In a huff. Returning for Isaac and her things. Ready to leave for the evening—

JORY: Isaac, we need to get out of here—

—but stopped in place by the moment of intimacy between her husband and Emily.

ISAAC: Honey?

JORY: What the fuck is going on here?

Amir enters, inflamed.

AMIR: You wait a week to tell me this? And the second I say something you don't like hearing, you walk away from me in mid-fucking sentence?

Who *are* you?!

Jory just stares at her husband...

AMIR (CONT'D): What?

(Looking around)

What?

JORY *(To Emily)*: Are you having an affair with my husband?

AMIR: Excuse me?

ISAAC *(To Jory)*: Nobody's having an affair.

JORY: I walked in here and they were kissing.

EMILY: That is not true! Amir, it's not true.

JORY: They were kissing.

(Pointing)

There.

EMILY: That's not what was happening.

JORY: I know what I saw.

EMILY: Isaac told me about them making you partner. I know how much longer Amir has been there than you. I was upset. I was crying.

ISAAC: I was consoling her.

JORY: By kissing her?

EMILY *(Incredulous)*: We weren't kissing! Why do you keep saying that?!

JORY *(To Isaac)*: Are you having an affair with her? Tell me the truth.

ISAAC: Honey. I already said. We're not having an affair.

JORY: So *what the fuck* were you doing when I walked in here?

ISAAC *(Going to his wife)*: I was hugging her because she was crying.

JORY: Get off me!

EMILY: I was upset they made you partner.

I know how much longer Amir has been there.

I was crying.

Amir turns to Jory. Vicious.

AMIR: First you steal my job and now you try to destroy my marriage? You're fucking evil. After everything I've done for you?

Jory goes over to get her purse. As if to leave.

JORY: I know what I saw.

AMIR *(Exploding)*: You have any idea how much of myself I've poured into that place? That closet at the end of the hall? Where they keep the cleaning supplies? That was my first office!

Yours had a view of the fucking park!

Your first three years? Were you ever at work before anyone else in the morning?

Were you ever the last one to leave?

Cause if you were, I didn't see it.

I *still* leave the office after you do!

You think you're the nigger here?

I'm the nigger!! Me!!

ISAAC *(Going to his wife)*: You don't need to listen to any more out of this asshole.

JORY *(To Isaac)*: Don't touch me.

AMIR *(To Isaac)*: You're the asshole.

ISAAC: You better shut your mouth, buddy!

AMIR *(To Isaac)*: Or what?!

ISAAC: Or I'll knock you on your *fucking* ass!

AMIR: Try me!

JORY *(To Isaac)*: GET OFF ME!!

> *Inflamed, Isaac finally releases his wife, facing off with Amir.*
>
> *When suddenly—*
>
> *Amir spits in Isaac's face.*
>
> *Beat.*
>
> *Isaac wipes the spit from his face.*

ISAAC: There's a reason they call you people animals.

> *Isaac turns to his wife.*
>
> *Then turns to Emily.*
>
> *Then walks out.*

AMIR *(To Jory)*: Get out.

JORY *(Collecting her things)*: There's something you should know.
Your dear friend Mort is retiring.
And guess who's taking over his caseload? Not you. Me.
I asked him, *Why not Amir?*
He said something about you being duplicitous.

That it's why you're such a good litigator. But that it's impossible to trust you.
(At the door)
Don't believe me?
Call Mort. Ask him yourself.
Let me guess.
He hasn't been taking your calls?

Jory walks out.

Pause.

EMILY: Have you lost your fucking mind?!

Amir turns away, withdrawing into himself. Pacing. The inward spiral deepening.

EMILY (CONT'D): Amir!
AMIR: She's right. He hasn't been taking my calls.
EMILY: I'm gonna get you that coffee.

Emily heads for the kitchen...

Leaving Amir onstage by himself for a moment. As he watches the swinging door sway. Back and forth.

Emily returns. A mug in hand.

AMIR: Em.

Something in Amir's tone—vulnerable, intense—stops her in place.

AMIR (CONT'D): Are you sleeping with him?

Pause.

Emily puts the mug down on the table.

Beat. Finally shakes her head.

EMILY: It was in London. When I was at Frieze.
We were drinking. It's not an excuse...
It's just...
We'd just been to the Victoria and Albert. He was talking about my work.
And...

Emily—seeing how her words are landing on her husband—makes her way to him.

EMILY (CONT'D) *(Approaching)*: Amir, I'm so disgusted with myself. If I could take it back.

All at once, Amir hits Emily in the face. A vicious blow.

The first blow unleashes a torrent of rage, overtaking him. He hits her twice more. Maybe a third. In rapid succession. Uncontrolled violence as brutal as it needs to be in order to convey the discharge of a lifetime of discreetly building resentment.

(In order for the stage violence to seem as real as possible, obscuring it from direct view of the audience might be necessary. For it to unfold with Emily hidden by a couch, for example.)

After the last blow, Amir suddenly comes to his senses, realizing what he's done.

AMIR: Oh, my God...

Just as...

There's a KNOCKING at the door.

Beat.

And then more KNOCKING.

Finally, the door gently opens. To show:

Abe.

Abe looks over and sees—as we do—Emily emerge into full view, on the ground, her face bloodied.

Abe looks up at Amir.

Lights Out.

Scene Four

Six months later.

The dining table, a couple of chairs.

Much of the furniture gone. The rest of the room covered with the detritus of moving. Boxes, etc.

The painting above the mantel is gone.

Along one wall leans a smaller, partially wrapped canvas. It is turned away from the audience.

As the lights come up, Amir is on stage. Quietly going about the process of packing. There should be something muted about his movement/presence. As if a man chastened by life, perhaps even crippled inwardly.

He has a thought and heads for the kitchen. Just as he exits, there is a KNOCKING at the front door . . .

He reemerges. Crossing and going to the door. He opens to find:

Emily. And, to one side, Abe. Abe is wearing a Muslim skullcap. And his wardrobe is muted. Unlike the vibrant colors of the first scene.

AMIR: Em?

EMILY: Can we come in?

AMIR: Of course.

They enter.

Abe appears reluctant. Not meeting Amir's gaze.

AMIR (CONT'D): What's going on here? Everything all right?

EMILY: Not really.

AMIR: What?

Emily looks at Abe, but Abe doesn't respond.

AMIR (CONT'D): Huss?

No response.

Amir turns to Emily, making a gesture toward her, not even realizing it...

AMIR (CONT'D): Em?

EMILY *(Recoiling)*: No, please.
   (Beat)
   He's been coming to me. You need to hear this.
   (To Abe)
   Tell him.

ABE: He's not going to understand.

EMILY: He got stopped by the FBI.

AMIR: What?

ABE: I didn't get stopped.

AMIR: What happened?

EMILY: Just sit down and tell him.

AMIR: What happened?

ABE: I didn't get stopped. All I was doing was sitting in Starbucks...

EMILY: With your friend...

AMIR: Don't tell me...Tariq?

ABE: Yeah.

AMIR: Hasn't everybody been telling you—

EMILY *(Coming in)*: Let him speak.

ABE: My parents are wrong about him.

AMIR: Okay.

ABE: We were at Starbucks. Just drinking coffee. Tariq starts talking to this barista who's on break. I can tell she's not into him. He's not getting the message...She starts asking about our kufi hats and are we Muslims. And then she asks us how we feel about Al-Qaeda. So Tariq tells her. Americans are the ones who created Al-Qaeda.

(Off Amir's look)

You don't believe me?

AMIR: That's not really the—

ABE: The CIA trained the mujahideen in Afghanistan. Those are the guys that became Al-Qaeda.

AMIR: I mean, it's a little more complicated than that—

ABE: Actually, it's not, Uncle. Not really.

AMIR: Okay. What happened?

ABE: So she got snippy. And Tariq got pissed. He told her this country deserved what it got and what it was going to get.

(Pause)

She goes back to work, and before we know it, the police are there. She called them. They cuff us. Take us in. Two guys from the FBI are at the station, waiting.

(Beat)

We sit through this ridiculous interrogation.

AMIR: What did they ask you?

ABE: Do we believe in jihad? Do we want to blow stuff up? How often did I read the *Koran*?

AMIR: Okay...

ABE: Do we have girlfriends? Had I ever had sex? Do I watch porn? Do I hate America?

(Beat)

They knew a lot about me. Where I'd gone to school. About Mom and Dad, where they were born. Like they already had a file.

They brought up my immigration status.

AMIR: What about it?

EMILY: It's up for renewal.

ABE: When they said that...

(Hesitating)

...I laughed.

AMIR: You laughed?

ABE: I didn't mean to. It just happened.

AMIR: Were you trying to antagonize them?

ABE: No.

I mean...

(Pause)

Look. I know what they're doing.

AMIR: What are they doing?

ABE: They're going into our community and looking for people whose immigration status is vulnerable. Then they push us to start doing stuff for them.

AMIR: Okay...

ABE: So what? You don't believe that either?

AMIR: I didn't say that.

Pause.

EMILY *(Suddenly moving off)*: I'm gonna go. He needed to talk to
you...

AMIR: Where are you going?

ABE *(Standing)*: Aunt Emily. Stay. Please.

She stops.

Beat.

Finally nods, still reluctant.

EMILY: I'm gonna get some...water.

Emily crosses to the kitchen. Exits.

Beat.

AMIR: Is she okay?

ABE: I don't want to talk about that.

Amir starts dialing on his phone.

ABE (CONT'D): Who are you calling? You can't call Mom. She's
gonna freak out.

AMIR: I'm calling Ken.

ABE: Ken?

AMIR: The lawyer on Imam Fareed's case...
   (Into the phone)
   Hi, Ken, it's Amir. Please call me back when you get this.
It's urgent. Thanks.
   (Pause, then to Abe)
   When you step out of your parents' house, you need to
understand that it's not a neutral world out there. Not right

now. Not for you. You have to be mindful about sending a different message.

ABE: Than what?

AMIR: Than the one that landed you in an interrogation with the FBI.

Pause.

ABE: So now what?

AMIR: Let's hear what Ken has to say. I mean, it's not good. But at least they let you go.

ABE: If he tells me that I have to go into our mosque and pretend I'm planning some bullshit attack just to stay in this country—

AMIR: You don't know that's what's going to happen.

ABE: If you spent any time with your own people...

AMIR: Excuse me?

Beat.

ABE: What would you do? If the FBI asked you to work for them? Hmm?

AMIR: We're not there yet...

ABE *(Cutting him off)*: What would you do?

AMIR *(Considering)*: There are ways...to let the authorities know that...you're on their side...

ABE: But I'm not on their side.

AMIR: You might want to rethink that. Because they make the rules.

ABE: I knew this was a mistake.

AMIR: It's not a mistake. If you're not smarter about this, you are going to get deported.

Beat.

ABE: Yeah, well, maybe that wouldn't be the worst thing.

AMIR: To a country you haven't known since you were eight years old.

ABE: Maybe that's the problem. Maybe we never should've left. Maybe we never should have come to this one.

AMIR: There's a reason your father came here. Same reason my father did. They wanted to make a better life for themselves and their families—

ABE *(Over)*: A better life?!?

AMIR *(Continuing)*: —and to do it honestly. Which isn't an option in Pakistan.

ABE *(Exploding)*: You don't have a better life!

AMIR: What are you talking about?

ABE: I know you were fired!

AMIR: I don't know what you think you know—

ABE *(Quiet, intense)*: I know what you did to her. How could you?

Beat.

AMIR: I don't know.

Beat.

ABE: You want something from these people you will never get.

AMIR: I'm still your elder. You need to show me a little respect.

ABE: Just because I'm telling you the truth doesn't mean I'm not showing you respect.
(Beat)

You forgot who you are.

AMIR *(Triggered)*: Really? *Abe Jensen?!*

ABE: I changed it back!

AMIR: So now you think running around with a kufi on your head, shooting your mouth off in Starbucks, or sitting in a mosque and bemoaning the plight of Muslims around the world is going to—

ABE *(Interrupting)*: It's disgusting. The one thing I can be sure about with you? You'll always turn on your own people. You think it makes these people like you more when you do that? They don't. They just think you hate yourself. And they're right! You do!

I looked up to you. You have no idea—

AMIR: No. I know.

ABE: No! You have no idea what it did to me!

(Beat)

I mean, if you can't make it with them...?

(Having a dawning thought)

The Prophet wouldn't be trying to be like one of them. He didn't conquer the world by copying other people. He made the world copy him.

AMIR: Conquer the world?

ABE: That's what *they've* done.

They've conquered the world.

We're gonna get it back.

That's our destiny. It's in the Quran.

We see Emily appear at the swinging door, listening.

Abe doesn't notice her.

84

ABE (CONT'D): For three hundred years they've been taking our land, drawing new borders, replacing our laws, making us want be like them. Look like them. Marry their women.

They disgraced us.

They disgraced us.

And then they pretend they don't understand the rage we've got?

Emily emerges.

Abe realizing she has heard him.

Abe moves to the door. Stops. Looks back at Emily.

ABE (CONT'D): I'm sorry.
AMIR: Hussein...
ABE: I'll handle it myself, Uncle.

Abe exits.

Leaving Amir and Emily.

Silence.

AMIR: My sister's been telling me about him...I didn't realize...
 (*More silence*)
 Are you reading my letters?
EMILY: Amir...
AMIR: I got the painting.
EMILY: I didn't want to throw it out.
AMIR: There was no note...
 (*Beat*)
 Look, I told your lawyer I wanted you to have the apartment. I mean, I wrote you that, but I have no idea if—

EMILY: The apartment's not mine.

Beat.

AMIR: If you hate me so much, why did you drop charges?
EMILY: I don't hate you, Amir.

Pause.

AMIR: I saw the write-up in *The New Yorker*. I was so proud of you.
EMILY: Oh.

Pause.

AMIR: I don't know if you've read any of my letters... There's a lot you were right about me.
    I'm finally seeing what you were seeing.
    I'm finally understanding your work.
EMILY: My work was naive.
AMIR: No, it wasn't. Why are you saying that?
EMILY: Because it's true.
AMIR: God. If you had any idea how sorry I am.
EMILY: I know.

Emily crosses. Stopping when she gets to the door.

EMILY (CONT'D): I had a part in what happened.
AMIR: Em. No.
EMILY: It's true.
    (Beat)
        I was selfish.
        My work...
        It made me blind.

AMIR: I just...
> *(Long pause, Amir emotional)*
>> I just want you to be proud of me.
>> I want you to be proud you were with me.

Beat.

EMILY: Good-bye, Amir.
>> Please. Don't write me anymore.

She exits.

Long beat.

As Amir walks over to return to packing, he notices...

The partially wrapped canvas against the wall.

He walks over to it, picks it up. Then tears the rest of the wrapping off. From his position on stage, we will only see enough of the painting to realize:

It is Emily's portrait of him. Study After Velázquez's Moor.

He takes a searching long look.

Lights Out.

AN INTERVIEW WITH
AYAD AKHTAR

Ayad Akhtar talks with Madani Younis, artistic director of the Bush Theatre in London, where *Disgraced* opened in May 2013.

(A version of this interview originally appeared in the July/August 2013 issue of *American Theatre* magazine, published by Theatre Communications Group.)

MY: Last day in London. How are you feeling?

AA: Great. It was a very intense experience working with the cast here and the director. The play grew. For me, the outstanding dramaturgical issues that needed attention were addressed. And of course, the production turned out wonderfully.

MY: What did the play in London reveal to you that you hadn't seen before?

AA: Nadia Fall brought a heightened quality, a ceremoniousness that was very different from the ease, the lightness of the New York and Chicago productions. Nadia's production was appropriate for the London audience, where the theatrical space is more ritu-alized. Theater has a long, living tradition here as an art form. The feel of the London production was very different from those in the United States, where stage presence has to mirror film and TV presence to feel convincing. Kimberly Senior's productions were wonderful, and right for the American audience. Different versions for different audiences. That's probably as it should be.

MY: You recrafted scene 4 of *Disgraced* for this version. Why?

AA: One of the issues I was continually having with *Disgraced* over the last couple of years was the transition out of scene 3 into scene 4. I would sit in the audience in New York and feel that, after the intensity of the events in the third scene, the audience was still very much with the act of violence. We would start the fourth scene in a very tangential, narrative way, not clear what the connection was to what we'd just seen. And that connection wouldn't be made clear for ten minutes. It was a long speed bump, during which I would feel some audience members shifting in their seats, like they were wondering what exactly was going on. It always seemed to me if there was a way to bridge that gap, to transition more viscerally, then we could get right to the meat of the fourth scene without the hiccup. The possibility of Abe com-ing in at the end of the third scene, as he does now, and then Emily and Abe showing up together at the beginning of the fourth solved the dilemma for me.

MY: This play is on at the moment here at the Bush Theatre, and it's set box office records for us. We opened this show with an 80 percent advance on ticket sales over a seven-week run, which was unprecedented. Talk to me a little about your observations about a British audience confronting *Disgraced*.

AA: There's an equal intensity of engagement, but it almost feels like the British audience is giddy with excitement at the end of the show. Jazzed. Not that they don't go through the troughs and the emotional shattering; I mean, I've seen quite a few people wiping away tears, and I'm hearing the shocked gasps at the play's key moments. But there's an ebullience at the end of the show that feels different from New York, where there was a similar intensity, but a kind of quiet, a deep sadness, something much more recognizable as a response to tragedy....

MY: What have your conversations with audience members at the end of the show been like? How do you think this play has connected with them?

AA: There've been two kinds of reactions. One is people coming up to me to acknowledge that they've had a meaningful and emotional experience. They often share that in a physical way, a facial way, and there isn't too much commentary. And then there's another reaction, having to do with the trouble the play seems to release into the audience, the folks who come up to me and ask point-blank what it is I'm trying to say. Because the play has not resolved that for them.

MY: Watching that is what's fascinating. The play is a provocation. It is not a singular point of view that one needs to acknowledge. It's not earnest in that regard; it's far more complex.

Let us for a moment talk about the violence in the play that is perpetrated by Amir upon his wife, Emily. What does that moment mean?

AA: Well, I want it to mean different things. It's obviously playing into certain Islamophobic tropes. I want the audience to be so fully humanly identified with a protagonist who acts out in an understandable but tragically horrifying way, that no matter what text you put on top of it, you cannot dissociate yourself from him. So even if you put that Islamophobic text on top of it, it doesn't change his humanity. That's the subtlest level. But there are other levels as well. The psychological; the gender relationship in its religious dimension on the one hand, in its modern Western dimension on the other; and of course, the way in which what Amir does is an act of political violence, that is to say a colored male subject who is acting out on a white female love object through violence, and in a way rife with political valences. In that respect the play is drawing on a tradition of representation: Shakespeare and V. S. Naipaul and William Faulkner. I wanted Amir's act of violence to be in dialogue with the acts of violence defined by that lineage. One of the things that's problematic about the play to a lot of people is that certain readings of the play seem to undermine other readings. And so the question becomes, well, what *is* the reading of this play? My contention is that your reading of this play tells you a lot about yourself. And I'm reminded of that wonderful thing Rainer Werner Fassbinder, the New Wave German filmmaker, once said, about how he wished to create a revolution not on the screen but in the audience. One way you can do that is by offering something that is so troubling, so multivalent, that the people in the audience cannot easily answer or release the questions that the piece has raised for them. They remain compelled, even despite themselves, to continue trying to make sense of what they've seen. Inspired by Fassbinder, I would say: The play's resolution lies not onstage, but in the consciousness of the audience.

MY: A hypothetical question, but one I feel duty bound to ask: What would the play become if it did not have the violence we witness between Amir and Emily? For that scene could occur with Amir walking out and leaving Emily standing alone in that space. What does that version of the play look like?

AA: I think that play is much more concordant with contemporary dramaturgical practice. Indirection, attention to the mundane, thwarted action. Those are qualities in some plays, but that's not the play I wanted to write. I wanted to engage the audience in a way that was much more fundamental, more primal than the contemporary approach to catharsis allows. We often forget that Greek tragedy was a mass form, and a religious one at that, very different in emotional tenor to the detached, noble quality of modern tragedy. The kind of vital emotional and intellectual engagement I long to establish with the audience requires closing the distance between the play and its viewers. *Disgraced* draws on melodrama, potboiler, romantic thriller, situation comedy, because one way to close that distance is to have the audience relating to the play not as an object of art but as something closer to an entertainment.

MY: Let us just go back for a moment to interpretation and the ideas of interpretation. This play had its press night here at the

Bush Theatre this past Wednesday, and in the last forty-eight hours, we have been inundated with some across-the-board very, very strong reviews from our newspapers. We're seeing right-wing papers referring to this through a very particular lens toward Islam, and we're seeing the left-wing papers referring to this in a far gentler, accessible sense. What has that made you think?

AA: That's been my experience with this play in general. Again, my feeling was that in order to do what I wanted effectively—which was to connect viscerally with the audience—I had to do it in a way that was unmediated by the interpretive layers. After the fact, each member of the audience is going to scour their experience of the play for clues, but after all is said and done, they will end up using their own categories to understand what they've experienced. So it makes perfect sense to me that people would gravitate to whatever reading feels most familiar to them. Ultimately it doesn't really matter, because there's another kind of space that's been opened up. An emotionally rich space, a space where opposing points of view, opposing readings of the play, can coexist. The success or failure of the play, as far as I'm concerned, rests in how alive that multivalent space is for an audience member. Let me give you an example. There was a Scottish-born Muslim woman of Pakistani descent who came to see the show a couple of nights ago who wrote me an e-mail saying, "It's been two days since I've seen it, and I'm still deeply troubled. I find myself walking through the streets in a different kind of depression than I've experienced before, wondering what people are really thinking and really is there hope for the future?" On one level I could say: "Wow, that was a real downer. Why did I write a play that is such a downer?" Or on another level, though, we could say she has dropped down to another, deeper state of reflection about where the world is. A confrontation with the recalcitrant tribal tendencies we all harbor. That kind of clarity of vision—or openness to the possibility of clearer vision—this is the sort of thing for which I'm hoping the play can be a portal. Look, at the end of the day, art's capacity to change the world is profoundly limited. But what it can do is change the way we see things individually. I aspired to accomplish with this structure a kind of shattering of the audience, after which they have to find some way to put themselves back together.

MY: Let me ask you, then, in response to what you've just said: Is the play hope*ful* or hope*less,* from your perspective as the playwright?

AA: I'm not sure that it's either. What it is, I hope, is an access point to a state of presence.

MY: For those in the world of the play, is there hope at the end of the play?

AA: I would repeat: I believe that in Amir's case, as well as Emily's case, and in his own way Abe as well, the events of the play have provided access to the present—to things as they are. That's the only way we can change anything, the only way we can change ourselves. The only way we can change the world is by recognizing what it is, now.

MY: Let's move on to my final question. As you know, I myself am Muslim, I'm Sufi, I'm British born. This is home. This country is home for me. For young Muslims who encounter this play, I can imagine they are surprised by the character of Amir.

AA: Sure.

MY: What are the thoughts that you leave young Muslims with about this play?

AA: It's a problematic, complex, deeply troubling play. I'm not going to avoid that. What I would say is that the concussive impact of its very economical ninety minutes belies a complexity of design on a metaphorical level. The play begins with a Western consciousness representing a Muslim subject. The play ends with the Muslim subject observing the fruits of that representation. In between the two points lies a journey, and that journey has to do with the ways in which we Muslims are still beholden on an onto-logical level to the ways in which the West is seeing us. And what the play might be suggesting is that we are still stuck there. The play ends with Amir finally confronting that image. I *do* believe personally that the Muslim world has got to fully account for the image the West has of it and move on. To the extent that we con-tinue to try to define ourselves by saying, "We are *not* what you say about us," we're still allowing someone else to have the domi-nant voice in the discourse.

ACKNOWLEDGMENTS

I have so many to thank, and short mention here is certainly not thanks enough for all they have given: Judy Clain, Terry Adams, Nicole Dewey, and everyone else at Little, Brown who made this edition happen. My brilliant and committed agents, Chris Till and Donna Bagdasarian. Amanda Watkins, who found this play and has shepherded it with care and intelligence at every stage of the process. Paige Evans, Andre Bishop, and everyone at LCT3, for their tireless enthusiasm and understanding of the artistic process. Kimberly Senior, my co-collaborator in so many senses. Marc Glick, as ever. Nils Folke Anderson, who brought to life Emily's art in Chicago, New York, and London. Matthew Rego and Hank Unger, guides and mentors at every stage of this play's birth and development. Madani Younis and the Bush Theatre, a brother and a home away from home. P.J. Paparelli and the American Theater Company, where the play started. And of course, Michael Rego and the rest of the Araca Group.

I benefitted from early readings of the play and have so many to thank for those opportunities: Firdous Bamji, Bill Camp, Florencia Lozano, Cassie Freeman, Nicole Galland, Brooke and Brian Ditchfield, Amy Barrow, Ed Vasallo, Webb Wilcoxen and the Labyrinth Theater Company, Caitlin Fitzgerald, Yolanda Ross,

Kevin Geer, Jason Pugatch, Miriam Hyman, Georgia Lyman, Ashley Melone at Vineyard Arts Project, Annie Parisse, Eisa Davis, Maria Dizzia, Matt Rauch, Manish Dayal, Quincy Tyler Bernstein, Shaz Khan, Brenda Barrie, Daniel Cantor, Kareem Bandealy, Adam Poss, Alison Mack, Adam Dannheiser.

The amazing casts of the first three productions, who taught me so much about this play: Usman Ally, Lee Stark, Alana Arenas, Benim Foster, Behzad Dabu, Heidi Armbruster, Karen Pittman, Erik Jensen, Omar Maskati, Hari Dhillon, Kirsty Bushell, Nigel Whitmey, Sarah Powell, and Danny Ashok. And of course, Aasif Mandvi, for his steadfast support and inspiration at every stage of this process.

Finally, to those whose contributions, personal and professional, were essential: Don Shaw, Ami Dayan, Steve Klein, Maria Semple, Michael Pollard, Shazad Akhtar, David Caparelliotis, Dan Hancock, Elise Joffe, Jim Nicola, JT Rogers, Joel de la Fuente, James Lapine, Sarah Kernochan, Stuart Rosenthal, Polly Carl, Seth Gordon, David Van Asselt, Oren Moverman, Poorna Jagannathan, Cathryn Collins, Sean Sullivan, Shane LePrevost, Brett Grabel, Nicole Laliberte, Eduardo Machado, and Liz Engelman.

And finally, my parents.

ABOUT THE AUTHOR

Ayad Akhtar is a screenwriter, playwright, actor, and novelist. He is the author of a novel, *American Dervish,* and was nominated for a 2006 Independent Spirit Award for best screenplay for the film *The War Within.* His plays include *Disgraced,* produced at New York's Lincoln Center Theater in 2012 and recipient of the 2013 Pulitzer Prize for Drama. He lives in New York City.